There's a DOLPHIN IN MY SWIMMING POOL

Written By:
Mackenzie K Wertman

Illustrated By:
Ravin Kaur

First Edition 2021

Wertman, Mackenzie K, 1996
There's a Dolphin In My Swimming Pool / by Mackenzie K. Wertman – 1st ed.
p. cm.

Summary: A little girl goes on adventures with her imaginary dolphin friend.

Hardback ISBN: 978-1-952255-99-1
Paperback ISBN: 978-1-952255-98-4
{1. Animals – Fiction. 2. Sea Creatures – Fiction. 3. Friendship – Fiction.}

This book was written by: Mackenzie K. Wertman.
This book was illustrated by: Ravin Kaur.

Printed in the United States of America

Arbuckle Publishing House
arbucklepublishinghouse.com

mackenziekwertman.com

here's a dolphin in my swimming pool.
She loves to jump and play.
We love to sit and chit chat
and go on adventures every day!

I don't know how she got there
or why she will not leave,
but I have come to love her,
and I've named her Sandy.

She likes to keep me company,
and I pretend that I'm a whale.
Cause she has no toes like me,
just flippers and a tail!

We sometimes go on picnics
and layout in the sun.
Her favorite thing to do
is to swim fast while I run.

Other times we stay in the water
and play all sorts of games.
From beach balls to toy rings,
we'll play with them all day.

Sometimes she even comes inside,
and we have adventures in the tub.
That's when there are lots of bubbles
and all new types of fun!

She protects me from the sharks
that lurk within the deep
and even from evil pirates
that sail the bathroom seas.

Then we visit mermaids
and ride with them on waves!
And when we're done exploring,
we rest near the ocean's caves.

And when bath time is finished
and Sandy returns to the pool...
She visits me in my dreams
and even sometimes at school.

And if there ever comes a day
where we are kept apart,
I keep a list of new ideas
written on a chart.

But do not be sad,
for when I am away,
Sandy has other friends,
like killer whales and stingrays!

And when we are back together,
it's like we never were apart!
We go back to all our fun,
and joy fills our hearts!

Then when the night falls
and my mom says it's time for bed.
I kiss Sandy goodnight,
and she rubs her nose against my head.

Another day awaits tomorrow,
filled with lots of fun,
and when the sun rises in the morning,
she's the first place that I run.

It's fun to have a dolphin
living in your pool.
All my friends and family
think it's really cool!

Do you, too, want a dolphin
that lives inside your pool?
If you dream like I do...
You can have a Sandy too!

CPSIA information can be obtained
at www.ICGtesting.com
Printed in the USA
BVHW021541200721
612420BV00007B/957

9 781952 255991